HiPPoPoTaMUS
Stew AND OTHER SiLLY ANiMAL PoeMS

 by JOaN HoRToN

illustrated by JoANN AdiNoLFi

Henry Holt and Company

New York

THE CENTIPEDE

She found running shoes with stripes for racing,
Shoes of black and brown and blue,
High-topped shoes that needed lacing,
Dress-up shoes that looked like new.
Shoes with wheels for in-line skating,
Snugly shoes to wear at night,
Majorette shoes for parading,
Shoes that pinched and felt too tight.
Shoes for dancing, shoes for prancing,
Shoes to learn to tie a bow,
Shoes for dashing, shoes for splashing,
Shoes with room for feet to grow.
Shoes of every size and kind—
Even worn and patched shoes,
But never, ever could she find
One hundred that-all-matched shoes.

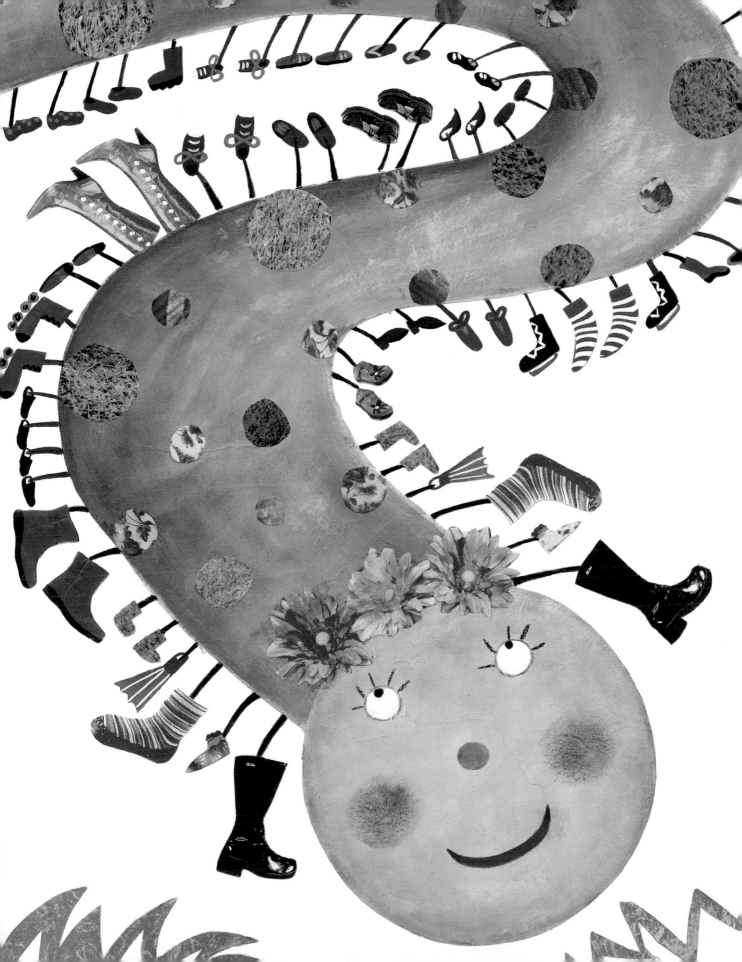

OLD MacDONALD'S BILLY GOAT

Old MacDonald's billy goat
Ate buttons off the scarecrow's coat,
An old tin can, some collard greens,
And one whole row of lima beans.
He gobbled up a length of twine,
Wet overalls right off the line,
A garden hose, an old straw hat,
A tractor bolt and after that
A spade, a hoe, a wooden rake,
A buzzing fly, for goodness' sake.
When nothing else was left to eat,
To chomp or chew or crunch,
He wandered to the farmer's house
And ate Big Mac for lunch.

The Jellyfish

A jellyfish washed up on shore
Followed by a dozen more,
Each one flavored like a berry,
Apple, guava, grape, or cherry.
"Wow," I heard my brother utter,
"Pass the bread and peanut butter."

The Flying Fish

A foolish fisherman from Maine
Seemed to think I was a plane.
He dropped his pole and hopped astride,
Then settled back to take a ride.
What a silly thing to do—
And him without a ticket, too.

The Snake

He slithered through underbrush, rubbed against bark,
And dragged across boulders from dawn until dark—
All in an effort to finally doff
The skin he was trying so hard to get off.
Then with a hiss the snake wearily said,
"The trouble I go through in order to shed!
How easily I could get rid of this skin
If only it came with a zipper built in."

HIPPOPOTAMUS STEW

Quickly, tell me, what would you do
If a hippo were stomping around in your stew,
Trampling on carrots and squashing the peas
And splashing the gravy clear up to his knees?
Would you say, "This is silly. Get out of my stew,"
And then cart the hippo right off to the zoo?
Or would you, perhaps, dip your spoon in your bowl
And scoop him right up and swallow him whole?

THE PENGUIN

The penguins, in their formal clothes,
Stood gathered on the icy floes.
"Ridiculous," the first one cried,
"You'd think a fellow'd have some pride."
The second nodded and concurred.
"Preposterous," chimed in the third.
The fourth one said, "Well, I declare,"
And couldn't help but stand and stare
The day they saw the penguin dressed
In checkered pants and flowered vest.

THE CHAMELEON

He awoke with a scream
From a terrible dream—
The worst one that he ever had.
Every leaf, every tree,
Every shrub, he could see,
Had turned from a green to a plaid.

THE ELEPHANT

How many tissues do you suppose
An elephant needs for a sniffly nose?
Does he need a couple, or three, or four,
A box, a carton, a gross, or ten score,
A truckload, a trainload, a big cargo planeload,
A million, a billion, a trillion—or two,
Or do you suppose that a trunkful would do?

THE CROCODILE

If ever you stroll on the banks of the Nile
And you happen to see an old crocodile smile,
Beware of his sly crocodilian grin—
There might be a napkin tucked under his chin.

The Sheep

With woolly fleece upon his back,
He's subject to a moth attack.
A nibble here, a munchie there,
And pretty soon the sheep is bare,
Which makes him look downright pathetic.
Too bad his fleece is not synthetic.

THE KANGAROO

Mother Kangaroo cried, "Ouch!"
When Junior jumped into her pouch.
"You're much too big," said Mrs. K,
"To ride around like this all day.
You'll have to find, I have a notion,
Some other means of locomotion."

I'm a Fierce and Fearless Dragon

I'm a fierce and fearless dragon
Breathing red-hot plumes of flame.
Knights for miles around all tremble
At the mention of my name.
My claws are sharp as sabers,
My fangs precision honed.
My wings are strong and sinewy,
My mighty muscles toned.
Each resounding roar I thunder
Makes the other dragons pale,
And I pulverize the boulders
When I lash out with my tail.
The earth beneath me rumbles
With each giant seismic stride.
And the tracks I leave behind me
Measure more than ten feet wide.
I'm a fierce and fearless dragon,
The fiercest one of all—
Dreamed the teeny tiny lizard
Who's a mere two inches tall.

The Whale

The whale has an ocean to use for a tub,
So why, when he's ready to rub-a-dub-dub,
Does he spout sprays of water high over his head,
Lather with sea foam, and shower instead?

THE PORCUPINE

Said the boy porcupine to the girl porcupine,
"I adore every quill on your sharp prickly spine."
He tenderly gazed at her sweet bristly face
And gathered her close in a loving embrace.
Just as he did, he cried, "Ouch! Dearest heart,
No one will ever—yikes!—tear us apart.
Tell me you love me—eow!—say it's true,
Because I am hopelessly stuck on—ow!—you."

The Hyena

Afraid your latest knock-knock joke
Will fail to get a laugh?
Then don't tell it to the elephant,
The emu, or giraffe.
Forget the hippopotamus,
And skip the crocodile
(Although this crafty creature
Has been known to crack a smile).
Don't waste it on the chimpanzee,
The lion in its lair,
The kangaroo, the cockatoo,
The yak, or mirthless bear.
The silly old hyena
Is the one you should go after,
'Cause when he hears your knock-knock joke,
He'll double up with laughter.

THE ANTEATER

The ants in the anthill all started to riot,
Demanding the anteater go on a diet.
The anteater cried, "This is simply absurd.
Why, everyone knows that I eat like a bird."
And then with a flick of her long, sticky tongue,
She zapped all the ants and ate every last one.

THE DUCK

Chickens peep, canaries sing,
Robins chirp, "It's spring, it's spring."
Warblers warble, pigeons coo,
Roosters cock-a-doodle-do.
Sparrows twitter, blue jays squawk,
Mynah birds and parrots talk.
Little ducks go quack, quack, quack,
But I can't seem to get the knack.
Perhaps I'd have a lot more luck
If I were not a rubber duck.

THE FIREFLY

Although he's flying through the dark,
He doesn't seem to mind
The only light he has to shine
Is back in his behind.

THE MOSQUITO

A skeeter lighted on my arm,
Insisting that it meant no harm.
"But while I'm here," it buzzed, "I might
Just take a teeny tiny bite."
"Bug off," I cried. "I'm not a snack,"
And gave that little pest a whack.
Too bad I missed 'cause off it flew,
Then circled back as skeeters do.
"Don't be like that," I heard it plead.
"A little bite is all I need."
"Then that is what you'll get," I said
And ate that pesky bug instead.

P.S. A skeeter's not nutritious,
But who cares? It tastes delicious.

To Diane, Ken, Jennifer, and Jeff, with a heart full of love
—J. H.

For my little creature lover, Hans, who's getting big
—J. A.

Henry Holt and Company, LLC
Publishers since 1866
175 Fifth Avenue, New York, New York 10010
www.henryholtchildrensbooks.com

Henry Holt® is a registered trademark of Henry Holt and Company, LLC.
Text copyright © 2006 by Joan Horton
Illustrations copyright © 2006 by JoAnn Adinolfi
All rights reserved. Distributed in Canada by H. B. Fenn and Company Ltd.

Library of Congress Cataloging-in-Publication Data
Horton, Joan.
Hippopotamus stew : and other silly animal poems | Joan Horton ;
illustrated by JoAnn Adinolfi.—1st ed.
p.   cm.
ISBN-13: 978-0-8050-7350-8
ISBN-10: 0-8050-7350-7
1. Animals—Juvenile poetry. 2. Children's poetry, American.
I. Adinolfi, JoAnn. II. Title.
PS3558.06984H57 2006   811'.54—dc22   2005012132

First Edition—2006 | Designed by Donna Mark
Printed in the United States of America on acid-free paper. ∞
10 9 8 7 6 5 4 3 2 1

The artist used gouache, watercolors, colored pencil, and collage
on watercolor paper to create the illustrations for this book.

"The Centipede" was first published in the September 1997 issue of *Ladybug*.